A Note to Parents and Caregivers:

With a focus on math, science, and social studies, *Read-it!* Readers support both the learning of content information and the extension of more complex reading skills. They encourage the development of problem-solving skills that help children expand their thinking.

 The PURPLE LEVEL presents basic topics and objects using high frequency words and simple language patterns.

 The RED LEVEL presents familiar topics using common words and repeating sentence patterns.

 The BLUE LEVEL presents new ideas using a larger vocabulary and varied sentence structure.

 The YELLOW LEVEL presents more challenging ideas, a broad vocabulary, and wide variety in sentence structure.

 The GREEN LEVEL presents more complex ideas, an extended vocabulary range, and expanded language structures.

 The ORANGE LEVEL presents a wide range of ideas and concepts using challenging vocabulary and complex language structures.

When sharing a content focused book with your child, read to find out facts and concepts, pausing often to restate and talk about the new information. The realistic story format provides an opportunity to talk about the language used, and to learn about reading to problem-solve for information. Encourage children to measure, make maps, and consider other situations that allow them to apply what they are learning.

There is no right or wrong way to share books with children. Find time to read and share new learning with your child, and pass on the legacy of literacy.

Adria F. Klein, Ph.D.
Professor Emeritus
California State University
San Bernardino, California

Editor: Jill Kalz
Designers: Abbey Fitzgerald and Tracy Davies
Page Production: Ashlee Schultz
Art Director: Nathan Gassman
Associate Managing Editor: Christianne Jones
The illustrations in this book were created digitally.

Picture Window Books
5115 Excelsior Boulevard
Suite 232
Minneapolis, MN 55416
877-845-8392
www.picturewindowbooks.com

Printed in the United States of America.

All books published by Picture Window Books
are manufactured with paper containing at least
10 percent post-consumer waste.

Library of Congress Cataloging-in-Publication Data
Blackaby, Susan.
The carnival committee / by Susan Blackaby ; illustrated by Ryan Haugen.
p. cm. — (Read-it! readers. Social Studies)
Summary: The students of Hill Street School are getting ready for their spring
carnival, and the third-grade class is making the flyers and maps, but when a big
mistake is made on the flyer, it threatens to spoil the day.
ISBN-13: 978-1-4048-2335-8 (library binding)
ISBN-10: 1-4048-2335-2 (library binding)
[1. Carnivals—Fiction. 2. Maps—Fiction. 3. Schools—Fiction.] I. Haugen, Ryan,
1972– ill. II. Title.
PZ7.B5318Car 2007
[E]—dc22   2007005363

The Carnival Committee

by Susan Blackaby
illustrated by Ryan Haugen

Special thanks to our advisers for their expertise:

Mark Harrower, Ph.D.
Assistant Professor, Department of Geography
University of Wisconsin, Madison

Adria F. Klein, Ph.D.
Professor Emeritus, California State University
San Bernardino, California

PICTURE WINDOW BOOKS
Minneapolis, Minnesota

The kids at Hill Street School were getting ready for their spring carnival. A few of Mrs. Parker's third graders were making a flyer and a map. The flyer would tell kids and their parents about the carnival. The map would show everyone where to play games, listen to music, eat lunch, and more.

"I'll take notes for the flyer, Mrs. Parker," said Logan. He got out a colored marker and a sheet of paper.

Mrs. Parker knew Logan's handwriting wasn't very neat. But taking notes would be good practice for him. "Thank you, Logan," she said with a smile. "First of all, be sure to tell kids to bring their parents."

Logan wrote down what Mrs. Parker said.

Mrs. Parker showed the class a large map of the school.

"To start, let's pick a spot for the information booth," she said.

"How about near the front doors?" Jin said. "The booth will be the first thing people see when they get to school."

6

"Good idea," Mrs. Parker said. She drew the letter *i* on the map and circled it. "This is called a symbol. Symbols are pictures, shapes, lines, or letters that stand for something else. On this map, the circled *i* stands for 'information.'"

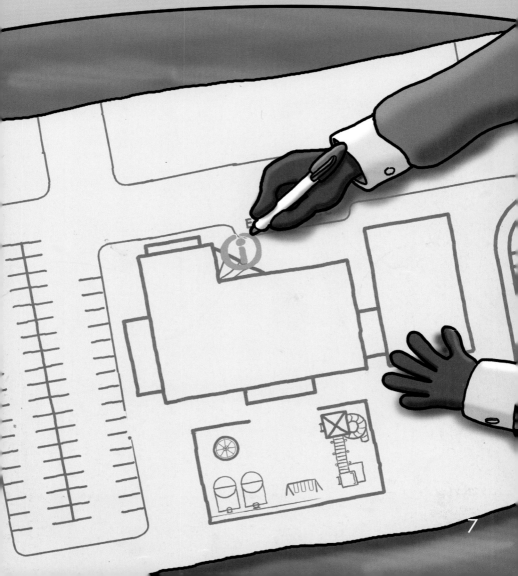

Rosa raised her hand. "Mrs. Parker?" she said. "*We* all know what the circled *i* stands for, but how will other people know?"

Mrs. Parker smiled. "We will add a key to the map," she said. "A key shows what all of the symbols on a map mean."

"That way, everyone will know what is what," Jin said.

"And everyone will know what is where," added Rosa.

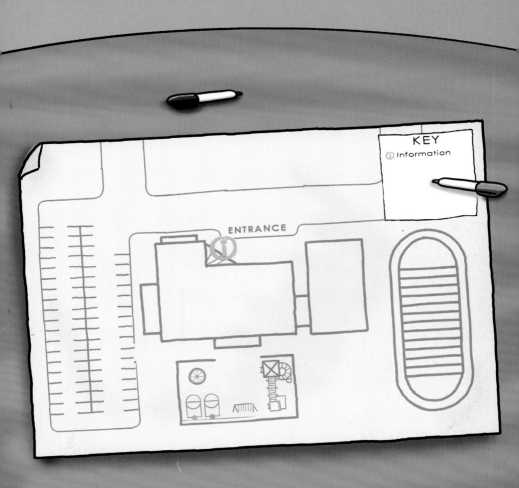

"Next, we need to pick a spot for the games," Mrs. Parker said.

"The gym would be perfect," Beth said. She drew a smiley face on the map. Then she added the symbol to the key.

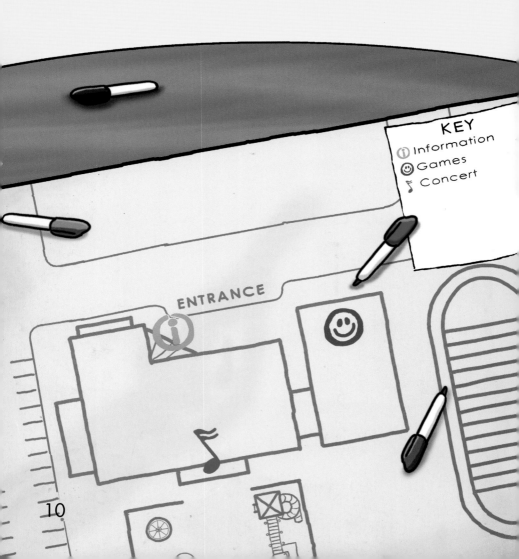

"Thank you, Beth," Mrs. Parker said. "The band is giving a concert at 10 a.m. We can put chairs in the music room and open the doors on the south side. Then people on the playground can hear, too."

Mrs. Parker drew a musical note on the map. Logan wrote everything down.

Rosa wrinkled her forehead. "How do we know which side is the south side?" she asked.

"We'll look at the compass rose," Mrs. Parker said. She drew something on the map that looked like a star.

"A flower will show us which way is south?" Rosa asked.

"A compass rose isn't a flower," Mrs. Parker said. "It's a symbol that shows direction. On this map, the compass rose shows the four cardinal directions: north—N, south—S, east—E, and west—W."

Mrs. Parker looked at her checklist. "Next on the list are the skateboard ramp and the first-aid station," she said. "Where should we put them?"

"The west parking lot is big enough for the ramp," said Jin. "Plus, it's close to the nurse's office. We could put the first-aid station there."

Mrs. Parker nodded, and Jin drew a ramp and a red cross on the map. Logan took notes.

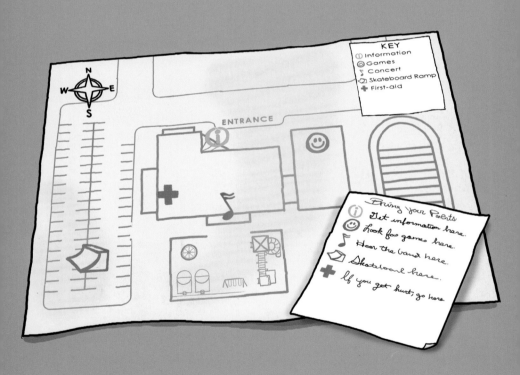

"Finally, we need to mark the track and the lunchroom," Mrs. Parker said. She drew a blue ribbon on the track. She drew a fork and spoon on the lunchroom. "The races will be on the track. Prizes will be awarded there, too. Food will be in the lunchroom."

Logan wrote down his final notes. Done!

Logan walked to the fourth-grade classroom. He gave his notes to a girl named Angie. Her job was to type them up and mail them.

Meanwhile, Beth, Rosa, and Jin hung the map up on the wall. They thought it looked great. Beth wrote the title of the map at the top. It said, "Hill Street Spring Carnival."

"Let's put this big map by the information booth," said Jin. "Then we can make smaller maps and put them all around the school."

Rosa cheered, "North, south, east, and west! Our spring carnival will be the best!"

On the day of the carnival, kids lined up at the information booth. They carried musical instruments. They carried skateboards and running shoes. They also carried dogs, cats, and other animals. One boy even had a snake.

Beth, Logan, Rosa, and Jin were puzzled.
"Why did so many kids bring a pet?" Rosa
asked. "And where are everyone's parents?"

Logan looked at the flyer. "Oh, no!" he cried. "There's a mistake! It was supposed to say, 'Bring your parents,' not 'Bring your pets!' My handwriting must have been too messy."

"Logan!" Rosa said. "What are we going to do with all of these pets?"

Bring Your Pets

Get information here.

Look for games here.

Hear the band here.

Skateboard here.

If you get hurt, go here.

Go to races and get awards here.

Eat here.

"I have an idea," Beth said, grabbing a marker. "We'll add them to the carnival. We'll have a pet parade! I'll draw the parade route on the map. Rosa, you go get Mrs. Parker."

Hill Street Spring Carnival

ENTRANCE

KEY
- ⓘ Information
- ☺ Games
- ♪ Concert
- Skateboard Ramp
- ✚ First-aid
- Races and Awards
- ✗ Food
- --> Parade Route

Beth drew a dashed line on the map. It started east of the information booth. It turned south between the school and the track. Then it turned west and looped around the playground. The line ended back at the track.

When Mrs. Parker got to the information booth, she saw all of the pets yapping and yipping, hissing and clucking. She shook her head and laughed.

Jin and Mrs. Parker lined up the pets. Logan asked two trumpet players to play a march. Rosa made a flag by tying a scarf to a branch. She and a parrot led the way.

The parade wound its way around the school. People cheered and clapped. The pet parade was the hit of the carnival.

At the end of the day, Principal Lyons gave out the prizes. There were awards for running and jumping. There was an award for the best skateboarding trick.

Mrs. Parker gave out a few special prizes. Angie, the fourth-grader, won the Boo-Boo on the Flyer Award. Logan won the Messiest Handwriting Award. Beth, Jin, Rosa, and Logan won the Map Whiz Team Award. "Without your map," Mrs. Parker said, "this place would have been a zoo!"

Dogs barked, cats meowed, and the snake hissed. The parrot cried, "Big day! Big day!"

"I just have one last thing," Principal Lyons told the noisy crowd. "I'm glad you brought your pets today. But next year, be sure to bring your parents, too!"

Activity: Making a School Map

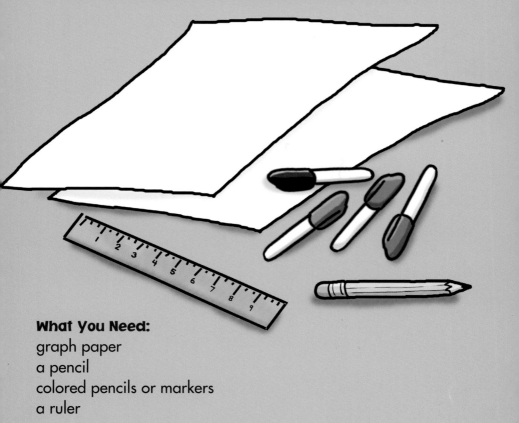

What You Need:
graph paper
a pencil
colored pencils or markers
a ruler

What You Do:
1. Using the map in this book as a guide, draw a map of your school. Use shapes to show where the buildings, the playground, the fields, and the parking lots are.
2. Mark the buildings and outdoor areas with symbols to show what they are used for.
3. Draw a key in the upper-right corner of your map to explain what the symbols mean.
4. Give your map a title, and show it to your parents. Can they find where you eat lunch? Play at recess? Wait for the bus?

Glossary

cardinal directions—the four main points toward which something can face: north, south, east, and west

compass rose—a symbol used to show direction on a map

key—the part of a map that explains what the map's symbols (for example, lines, shapes, and pictures) mean

symbols—things that stand for something else

title—the name of something, such as a book, movie, or map

To Learn More

At the Library

Leedy, Loreen. *Mapping Penny's World.* New York: Henry Holt, 2000.

Rabe, Tish. *There's a Map on My Lap!* New York: Random House, 2002.

Wade, Mary Dodson. *Types of Maps.* New York: Children's Press, 2003.

On the Web

FactHound offers a safe, fun way to find Web sites related to this book. All of the sites on FactHound have been researched by our staff.

1. Visit *www.facthound.com*
2. Type in this special code: 1404823352
3. Click on the FETCH IT button.

Your trusty FactHound will fetch the best sites for you!

Look for all of the books in the *Read-it!* Readers: Social Studies series:

The Carnival Committee (geography: map skills)
Groceries for Grandpa (geography: map skills)
Lost on Owl Lane (geography: map skills)
Todd's Fire Drill (geography: map skills)